Published in the UK in 2021 by Greenteeth Press

Content © the individual contributors, as credited
Typesetting © Imogen Peniston
Cover Design © Dan Hunt

All rights reserved. This book or any portion thereof may not be reproduced or used in any manner whatsoever without the express written permission from the publisher or individual authors, except for the use of brief quotations in a book review.

Printed in the United Kingdom.

GreenteethPress.com

Horrifying Tales

A Greenteeth Press and York Centre for Writing Anthology

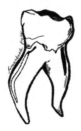

horrifying:

verb

To strike with fear (also scaring, scarifying, terrifying, terrorising)

Contents

Introduction *Dr Robert Edgar*	9
The Conductor *Paul Childs*	11
Haunted by Hedgehogs *Adam Ditchburn*	16
Flicker *Rob O'Connor*	17
Scared for Life *Clara Barley*	21
microdose diaries *Sam Jacques*	25
Sailors' Wives *Harrison Casswell*	32
The Tale of the Midnight Society *Jo Brandon*	34
The Slammer *Oliver J. Campbell*	35
Remember the Bear. *Errol-Graham Harsley*	39
No Strings Attached *Alan G. Smith*	41
But Emily Loved Him. *Claire Hinchliffe*	45
Home Again *Stella Miriam Pryce*	48
Spiders *Sarah Barr*	51
Three Matches *L Hudson*	52

Introduction

About three years ago I pulled my Denys Fisher Skull Machine from my parent's attic. Methylated spirits, carefully applied to the battery contacts by my father, coaxed the 43-year-old motor back to life. I stood with my daughter, then 11, and watched the Plaster of Paris pour its way round the orange mould, slowly forming the shape of a skull with deep hollow eyes and clenched teeth. This had been a Christmas present in the mid-1970s and was a feature in my bedroom wardrobe through to the early 1980s, an era where horror aimed at children was omnipresent; from the deeply unsettling *Pipkins*, through the terrifying *Children of the Stones* to the deeply eerie adaptation of the *Box of Delights*. This period is captured so evocatively by Ste Brotherstone and Dave Lawrence in *Scarred for Life* and by the writing of Bob Fischer at *hauntedgeneration.co.uk*. Reading their work made me realise that my desire to share these totems of my youth with my own daughter was not simply an act of nostalgia. The growing interest in the weird, eerie, and downright horrifying popular culture of the 1970s and 1980s was so powerful that it has shaped a generation. This was developed into an academic research interest with a collection of essays called *Horrifying Children* currently in publication. It was serendipitous that at the same time Greenteeth Press was born and had published the wonderfully unsettling anthologies, Pondweed and Unhomely. The two concepts came together in this collection of children's television inspired stories curated by Imogen at Greenteeth. They were due to be read at a symposium in York in 2020. For ongoing research, I was reading *Empty World* by John Christopher, a book that had entranced me in younger years. It is a tale of a deadly virus that sweeps the planet leaving a handful of survivors. As I finished re-reading Christopher's YA masterpiece the country started to lockdown and the conference was cancelled. I write this locked in my makeshift office space in my attic with only the odd spider for company after reading Imogen's Selection of stories and poems that will undoubtedly serve their purpose in horrifying and unsettling you. The Skull Machine is sitting in a corner begging me to open it one more time and for me to also create something truly horrifying.

Dr Robert Edgar
York St John University

The Conductor

Through thick fog we follow a lonely country railway flanked by steep, overgrown banks. A dark tunnel looms out of the mist. As we approach it we begin to make out figures through the haze.

"I am The Conductor," growls a deep, disembodied voice. We recognise it, but we're not sure where from. In the distance we hear sorrowful electronic music.

As the fog dwindles two motionless children fade into view, a boy and a girl. Their heads are bowed. A third, much taller individual lurks behind them, obscured by the gloom.

"Wherever there is a railway, you will find me, ready to help naughty children, the trespassers and the vandals make their connection."

A man with a thick moustache, wearing the uniform of an old fashioned railway guard steps out of the murk and towers over the children. He looks us in the eye, his unblinking gaze filled with fury.

He places a hand on the little girl's shoulder. She looks up at us. Her skin is so pale it almost seems blue. There is no life in her black eyes.

"Caroline's friends said she was too cowardly to take the shortcut across the railway. She proved them wrong and now they won't be teasing her ever again."

She bows her head again.

The Conductor ruffles the boy's hair. The emotionless child looks up at us.

"Keith lost his ball on the track."

The boy looks to his left. We see a black and white football lying in the ballast at the tunnel's entrance, the leather shredded and limp. Its burst bladder protrudes like the tongue of a dead animal by the roadside.

"I helped him find it..."

He takes a silver watch on a chain from his jacket pocket out and examines it.

"...and the 8.15 from Manchester."

He slots the watch back into his pocket.

We float towards him, through the tendrils of mist, getting closer, closer, until all we can see is the centre of his eye. Reflected in his impossibly black pupil is a steam train thundering towards us.

A whistle shrieks as steam and smoke from the engine violently swirl, merging with the mist until everything is white. The music swells as the fog clears. We see a grey platform crowded with pale, expressionless children. The carriage doors creak open.

"All aboard!" calls The Conductor.

The children shuffle onto the carriages. When the platform is empty the doors slam shut as one. The train pulls away and the shriek of its whistle fades to silence as the carriages are swallowed one-by-one by the tunnel's gaping mouth.

We back away from The Conductor until we see him glaring down his nose, pointing threateningly at us.

"Stay off the tracks," he says. "Or it's the end of the line for you."

He freezes, holding us in his malevolent stare. The words "RAILWAYS ARE NOT PLAYGROUNDS" appear in front of him. After a few seconds, everything fades to black.

The screen erupts in colour and sound. A jolly tune accompanies a gigantic bumblebee handing bowls of breakfast cereal to a pair of children who lick their lips excitedly…

****

"Charley, guess what?" Jimmy nudged his sister in the ribs.

"What?" she said.

"He's real, you know."

"What, Swarmy off the Nectar Nibbles advert? Nah! That's just a man in a suit," she said. "I might be only seven, but I'm not stupid."

"Not Swarmy, you idiot!" he said. "I meant The Conductor. He's real."

Charley laughed. "Don't be silly! He's not real!"

"He is!" Jimmy said. "I heard Rob's sister say her boyfriend saw him down by Graveling Tunnel last week."

"No you didn't! Shut up!"

Charley pouted. Jimmy smirked when he recognised the face she always pulled when she was about to cry.

As she began sniffing back tears Jimmy leaned in close to her ear. "He waits by the track and lures little brats like you down there and when you're close enough, he grabs you, and pulls you into the tunnel, which is like the gate to hell or something, and then he drives his train over you… forever."

"Mum!" Charley wailed. "Jimmy's scaring me again!"

"No I'm not, Mum! Charley's being a baby!"

"Enough, you two!" came a shout from another room.

"Charlotte, I've told you before, monsters are not real! And James, stop frightening your little sister. I'm busy and I haven't got the patience for your nonsense right now. Take her out to play somewhere, will you?"

"Aaaaah, Mum, that's not fair!"

"James Andrew Taylor! If you want to see that Lost Ark thing with your friends tomorrow then you will do this for me now."

"But…"

"No buts! And don't come back until teatime!"

"Fine!"

He stomped into the garden with Charley trailing behind. They retrieved their BMXs from the shed and mounted them, pedals raised ready to set off.

"W-where are we going?" Charley sniffed, wiping tears and snot away with the back of her hand.

"Dunno." He pushed off and slowly cycled toward the main road. He grinned and looked over his shoulder.

"I know what we can do!" he said.

"What!?"

"You'll see. Just don't be a slowcoach or I'll ditch you!"

Charley pedalled furiously to catch up.

"This'll be great!" Jimmy chuckled to himself.

****

The kids were never late for dinner. A knot of fear twisted in Mrs Taylor's stomach as she searched the phone book for the numbers of the other parents from school. She turned the TV volume down before making the first call and didn't hear the sorrowful electronic music of an old 1970s safety film.

****

"I am The Conductor," growls a deep, disembodied voice. "Wherever there is a railway, you will find me, ready to help naughty children, the trespassers and the vandals make their connection."

Two pale children step out of the mist and look up at us with cold, dead eyes.

"Jimmy's mother told him to look after Charley... But I took care of them both instead."

Paul Childs

Haunted by Hedgehogs

"Don't curl up"
Every time I cross the road
"Don't curl up"
I feel the fear in all my bones
"Don't curl up"
I see the wheels come rolling in
"Don't curl up"

Adam Ditchburn

Flicker

I walked past it every day on my way home from school. I thought of it as the House of the Dead, the fallen House of Usher, hummed the theme to *The Omen* as I walked past. It was surrounded by wizened trees, slightly hidden but visible enough from the road to be imposing. I longed to see inside its doors and find its skeletons.

But that day I was not thinking about the house, but rather who lived there. I was thinking about Beth.

Beth. Cute. Long, chestnut hair. I had liked her ever since her family moved into the House of the Dead. I'd had my chance in the summer but blew it. A typical teenage failed romance. It hadn't lasted long.

I had not seen Beth at school that day but had thought little of it, just assuming she was sick. The day had been uneventful, the normal routine of lessons, lunch and larking around. After the last lesson I headed out of school and into the gloomy winter afternoon. As I approached the house, I prepared myself for its foreboding appearance from the dark. It seemed empty, devoid of life. An upstairs window was faintly illuminated. As I passed, something caught my eye. Someone was standing at the window, staring out at the road.

It was Beth.

The figure was unmistakable, her frame backlit. I could see her facial features and her flowing hair, see the dim glow of the light on her skin. She was dressed in a long, plain night dress. Instantly, I felt regret. I had treated her badly. I was filled with the sensation of wanting to apologise, to talk to her. Impulsively, I waved.

That's when I suspected that something wasn't right.

She did acknowledge my action, nodding her head slightly.

Even from this distance I could feel there was something vacant about her demeanour, a deepness in her eyes. I'm not sure why, but somehow I felt she was trapped. Lost. It wasn't sadness. It was something else, something deeper. She was watching me, motionless. Eerie in her stillness.

I felt uneasy. I took a step back. I continued to watch her at the window, completely still, her stare cutting through me.

It seemed that I had been motionless for hours, but it was just seconds. I moved on but kept glancing back. She had shifted slightly, still visible in the window as I pressed on and eventually lost her in the skeletal frames of the surrounding trees.

I shook my head, feeling tense inside.

After a few steps, two shapes appeared side-by-side from the gloom, heading towards me. As the shadows formed into figures it became clear that it was a woman and a girl. I shifted slightly to give them both room to pass, lost in my own thoughts.

"Hiya." The voice was unmistakable. Sombre. Uncertain whether to speak or not.

I looked up in response and froze. It was Beth. Looking directly at me. Her hair lying across her shoulders. Her hazel eyes clear to see, alive and full of emotion. Her unexpected presence frightened me.

I had been scared before, several times. High up on clifftops, ready to abseil. Watching horror films. Yet this was different. It was visceral. It chilled me.

She saw my reaction and her expression turned puzzled. Her mother was next to her, holding Beth by the elbow.

"Everything okay?" Beth asked, looking at me.

It took a moment for me to respond. "How did you do that?" I asked.

"Do what?"

"I just saw you at the window in your house."

"No, you didn't." Beth replied. "I've been out with my mum all day. We're just getting back. I've been off school today. A family matter."

I looked back at Beth's house, peering through the surrounding trees at the upstairs window.

There was nothing there, but for a moment I thought I caught sight of a fleeting shadow and the light seemed to dim slightly. A flicker.

I turned back to Beth and met her eyes. Lost myself in them for a second.

"See you tomorrow," she said, as her mother led her onwards. It was somewhere between a question and a statement. I watched them as they moved into the shadows of the house.

I ran the rest of the way home. My hand shook as I tried to put the key in the keyhole.

In the silent sanctuary of my house I waited alone for my mum to return from work. I turned on the television to distract my thoughts and fill the living room with noise. *Round the Twist* was just starting, a show that I usually watched with glee. But not tonight. The show's playful theme music echoed around the dark living room: *Have you ever... ever felt like this?*
"No," I whispered into the shadows. "No, I haven't."

Strange things happen to us all the time. Moments we just cannot explain. Mostly you just shrug it off.

Yet sometimes... just sometimes... you can't...

Rob O'Connor

Scared for Life

It was something about the eyebrows made of wheat tips that stayed with me. Thirty years on. It wasn't him taking his head off. It wasn't having a rack of different heads to choose from. But the eyebrows. They're in there, scored in my brain, as vivid as any visions of my actual youth, along with the monkeys on wheels in *The Wizard of Oz,* the falling through the cracks in *Nightmare*, and all those things that sometimes pop into the forefront of your mind and send a shiver down your spine, which are never less than when you first saw them. Visions emblazoned deeply into your mind, never to be forgotten, out of context. But still as scary as they were for the pre-teen me who was determined to bravely watch everything my three-year older brother did. Unflinchingly. And not sleep for weeks. I also 'accidentally' saw Terminator aged eight. And the 'pin head' image on the video cover in the local video store, which is as burned on my retina as all the other horrifying visions.

As an adult, I don't watch horror. I avoid the genre at all costs. Largely, I think, because I was inadvertently exposed to so much of it as a child. My teenage and adult self now have enough images to haunt me forever. I knew, even by age fifteen, when asked if I wanted to watch *Halloween*, my answer was no. Definitely not. I already had a lifetime's worth of scary images and ideas ingrained in my mind's eye, so that all I wanted to watch was Disney.

Oh hang on, no, Disney terrified me too; Bambi's mum being shot! My poor mum had to remove her screaming children from the cinema (aged three and six). It was a U rating somehow. As was the aforementioned *Wizard of Oz.*

The *Snowman* melting! I must have been about four on first watching, far too young.

Watership Down? Commence fear of rabbits.

Rentaghost? Commence fear of ghosts. And weren't adults supposed to know better?

Jonny Briggs I only watched once as his parents, again, were SO scary. Someone even got trapped in a fridge! Bring on claustrophobia and a fear of large fridges for life. Thanks. They read like a list of childhood traumas.

Then there were clowns, puppet shows, masks, Halloween (least favourite day of the year). All best avoided. I could handle *Sesame Street*, *The Fraggles* and *The Muppets* (thankfully watched when old enough to know they were puppets) but *Legend* and *Labyrinth* were watched far too young at playschool and still haunt me. I even shuffle a bit uncomfortably watching Hobbits.

Another anxiety, this time of being left behind, I believe stems from the unicorn from *Dungeons and Dragons*, cleverly named Uni, who kept getting left behind. And instead of leaving the stupid creature they stayed to save him. Every. Single. Episode. In my dreams though, I was left behind.

I mainly stuck to cartoons; *SuperTed*, *Danger Mouse*, *Count Duckula* and *Duck Tales*, and the wonderful *Cities of Gold*. Which I think I truly believed was real, even though it was a cartoon, until one day on *The Broom Cupboard*, Phillip Schofield burst my bubble of childhood belief by saying the kid's hair was blowing in the opposite direction to the clouds in the opening credits. It was never the same for me again. Like discovering dad was Santa.

In hindsight, I also now note how few girls or women were in any of the cartoons. And if they did appear, they needed rescuing. I think my only heroines were Long Distance Clara in *Pigeon Street* and Cheetara from *ThunderCats*. As obviously, before the new millennia, only boys could have adventures.

Then in the 90s we drifted into *Neighbours*, *Byker Grove*, *Grange*

Hill, *The Really Wild Show* and *Blue Peter* and all that horrifying weirdness of kids' TV fell away and we were little grownups.

Books were somewhat easier to close and hide away, thus stopping the images fully forming, and you could stop reading and car boot sale the book or return to the local library to scare the bejeezers out of another unsuspecting child. I loved Roald Dahl (except for *The Twits*) as he managed to create 'enjoyable fear'- *The Witches* and the giants in *The BFG* were terrifying, but somehow, I felt in safe hands, I knew they would be redeemed. But *Five Children and It*? And the aptly named 'Scary' children's books? I'll stick to the *Tiger Who Came to Tea* please. *Lord of the Flies* at twelve years old anyone? *Flowers in the Attic*? I avoided the *Goosebumps* series and even *Horrible Histories*. There are some horrible historic facts I just don't want to read and never forget thanks.

Perhaps I just have a weak disposition for stories. I can't have house plants because of *Day of the Triffids* (compulsory school reading for this fourteen-year-old). I have to duck and weave around them when they are randomly in entrance ways and shops, just in case, you know...

So no, I do not watch, read, enjoy horror, any form of torture, anything that involves small spaces, fire, skeletons, masks, clowns, puppets, large fridges and am ridiculously squeamish. For although I'd tried to shield myself from all these things, unfortunately, even by my teenage years, the damage had been done. Horrific visions and ideas had been firmly implanted in my young mind.

Thank you children's TV, novel and film writers. Instead of inspiring me to undertake adventures and be brave, you made me scared of everything for life. Possibly even, scarred for life too. And you also failed to give me any heroines to aspire to be.

Don't mention *The Goonies*. A 'kids' film indeed! Terrifying. And no girls in that one either.

Clara Barley

microdose diaries

~~eggs~~

~~milk~~

~~angel delite~~

malt loaf   DOCTORS AT **2PM**!

~~cold sore~~

    DROP OFF MUMS

    SHOPPING TUESDAY

12.07.98

bagpuss trip:

    dossed in crabbies gaff after work. other side impendin. swan neked our reebok kwilted arms together. locked in a toast to learys drop out slobs. gobbed and diped. fused tip to tab, tab to tastebud.

saloo.

hours drifted into seepia like a wedding dj fondlin every 4 bars of a graveyard set.

1. please stop me now

2. if i could turn back time (itd sound like this)

3. dont let the sun go down on this gig

4. time warp

crabs pupils swalowed clang from the mortar driping tap. the room sinkholed sound. and our wispers swirled into it like dirty coppers in those shit ~~petril~~ petrol station coin swallers.

them that guzzle down ya seedy thrill into a suposed charity bucket whos name youv not even read.

fuckin scrached plastick hypnotics that. tossin ya beer money into governments urban fuckin wishin

well. wachin it white red its way into their greedy parms wile youre stood int cold. waitin on a

greased up bacon butty thatll only make ya pop ya clogs one day sooner. One day less them

                        bastards ull be pilferin my moolah.

watched neighbours for abit. thought trip ad settled after that.

THOUGHT FUCKIN RONG!

the most magical. the most beaotiful. soggy old dish cloth?

it wa bloody bagpuss.

but... not.

nails spiraled out of his paws. little black lice helter skeltered down his legs. shimmyin back up knots

        in pink and white dreds fer another go.

his body wheezed like that concert tina thing I saw on old grey

whistle test once (bob harris the
purring old twat).

he wa sickly celebs. he wa eazy-e. he wa sid viscious. he wa tommy coopers slapstick snuffin.

'em em emm emily emem emm emily' he dint shut up mutterin. he wa flownsin round ont coffee

table. wallowin in 3 day old tab ash like it wa the elixier a youth.

    rolled up a nutz mag and went rambo on him.

a coffee splatered pair of swinging double fs caught him across his snout.

after a coupla ding dings and a few complamentry stars flowtin round his head. he looked at me in silence. and spoke.

from bagism to bill clintons bit on the side ive seen it all. lingerd round collectin for emily.

pearly fuckin steam clouds risin in the air foldin into the drape of latherie whiff. like fujitiv deodrant serchin for an open window in a footie changin room.

i looked over for help and crabby was sparko soakin into the setee. sleep trippin the lazy cunt

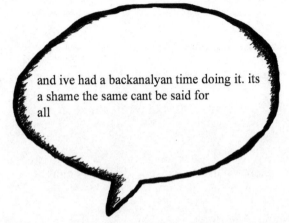

and ive had a backanalyan time doing it. its a shame the same cant be said for all

his fur erectd on his spine. sprawlin forward and touchin my knee. a haggered army of candy floss soldiers waiting for sobreness to disolve them back into the oblivyan of the past.

the fuse blew in the tv and valed us in greyness. the fumes waxed lyrical. and I could feel my eyes swell and puss as they were infectid with polutid words.

in life theres only one straw and its always short.
but one thing is constunt. i must collect.
and theres money in misery.

he gave a dictaters nod. and the mice apeard. they pinned me to the cushons. 2 on each limb. singing a choonless melody as they went. they were the rattling window as you hurtel down the moterway. they were feet dragging on the floor. they were a knife on a plate.

WE WILL FIND IT. WE WILL BIND IT

WE WILL STICK IT WITH GLUE GLUE GLUE

once I wa bound, they brought out the bodies.

lets finaly open the door. a lifes work in waiting

this is my mawsoleom...

the bloted carpet was a tomb of ~~apotles~~ aposles. eqally spaced in the middle of the room were the

rest of the bagpuss characters. each in a wicker basket with an epitaff at its feet.

proffessor yaffle – wise beyond the rings of the tree that made you.

madelin the ragdoll – stillnes was peice in both life and death.

gabriel the toad – never out of tune until he croaked it.

and directly in front of my puss stuck eyes. a empty caskit.

crab shook me. and the film burnt off the end of the reel.

mouse organ mice? stronger than they look.

epitaff? epitatt.

bagpuss? fuckin horder mate.

Sam Jacques

Sailors' Wives

Listen closely, children. I'm here to tell you a story. Now before I start, I want to make this crystal clear, I am not a children's entertainer. I do not want to be here. I am not here because it warms my heart to tell stories to babies. I am certainly not here for artistic integrity; I gave that up long ago. I am here because they are paying me to be here, to read to you. No other reason. Now, pay attention.

***

Once upon a time, long ago, long before you kids were born. In fact, I imagine before most of your parents were born. Once upon a time, there was a war. My father was a sailor in the navy during that war, I barely knew him. It was a war unlike those we know today. It wasn't fought from computer desks and remote command centres. This war was much different. Men had to go away from home. They had to leave their families behind, travel to strange lands and fight with guns and knives. It was a terrible war, for everyone involved. Especially the children. Left to grow up alone. A broken world, their inheritance. This story is about sailors. Or rather, it is about the families left behind.

Once upon a time, men crawled through the mud of foreign fields and tried to kill other men before they were killed themselves. Boats and warships crossed vast oceans and planes flashed in the sky. On the ground below, in British fields, on the shores of Britain – women and children waited for husbands to come home, fathers to come home. Many never did.

There are many stories to be told about the war. But for me, none are as interesting as the tales of sailors' wives.

Are you listening, children?

Once upon a time on a beach in the North of England, sailors' wives gathered together. They didn't speak, they didn't mingle, they just gathered quietly, night after night. Nobody is quite sure how this ritual started – or at least, I'm not. But I do remember the meaning behind it. The idea amongst the women was that as their men floated on distant waters, stars in the night twinkled above their ships. So they came to the beach. To look out above the sea, at the stars, in hopes that their husbands were looking up at the same sky. Somehow, looking at the stars made the distance between their men and the shores of home seem less significant. Some women would bring their children. They would guide their eyes to the night sky and tell them: Daddy's out there, underneath those stars, smiling, because he knows we're looking too. This ritual helped them all feel better, the emptiness in their lives didn't feel so vast next to the expanse of water and sky in front of them.

All except one, a blind woman named Joyce. Her eyes had ceased working a year before the war started. Her husband cared for her and their son, until the fighting began and he had to sail away. Her son did what he could to help her but he was only a child. It's hard to be the man of the house when you're eight years old. The strange thing about this story is that Joyce still went to the beach at night. She stood amongst the other women, gazing at nothing while her peers looked upwards. Every night she stood there and she felt nothing. She had nothing. No carer, no husband, no solace in the stars. I think she did it for her son. Waited on the beach, night after night, so that her son could witness the beauty that she was denied. So that he could feel closer to his father.

One night, for some reason – let's call it fate. Do you kids know that word, fate? The idea that everything happens for a reason. I'm here because I'm meant to be. You're here because you're meant to hear this story. Nonsense, in my opinion, but for the sake of the story, we'll suspend our disbelief.

Once upon a time, as fate would have it, a blind woman and her son stood closer to the water than usual. As fate would have it, the tide was higher this night than usual. The blind woman stood there, surrounded by other women and children, all gazing up at the stars. All but her found comfort in those distant lights. Those ethereal pin pricks of light that connected them with their husbands, who were away fighting the battles of more powerful men. As fate would have it, the sea rolled up the beach and kissed Joyce's toes. For the first time since her husband left, she felt something. A connection with him. She realised, like a switch had flicked on in her heart, what she must do. She may not be able to gaze at the stars above her man, but she can bathe in the waters that keep him afloat. She stepped forward, the water rolled in and again she felt that connection. She took another step. Another. Another. As she walked forwards, her son released her hand and watched his mother wade into the sea. She began to laugh and splash the water. Other women broke their concentration from the stars and watched, perplexed. She lay on her back and let the water take her out. The sea seduced her and once it had her, it never let go.

***

No response? No applause? Nothing, really? This is why I don't read to kids. Does anybody have a question for me, at least? What about you? Oh – I know what you want to ask.

He grew up to be a writer.

Harrison Casswell

The Tale of the Midnight Society

I wanted to be flame-scattered dust
I wanted to be ritual crackling as it burned
I wanted to be fear as it flared and rose
I wanted to be snapped branches in the woods
I wanted to be mist over black creek-shore water
I wanted to be old lake house piers and drifting row-boats
I wanted to be floorboards creaking in ruined mansions
I wanted to be dust-sheeted mannequins
I wanted to be the tattered ruff of a slash-mouthed clown
I wanted to be grinding rust on a disused swing set
I wanted to be a vacant merry-go-round — still turning
I wanted to be childish laughter from nowhere
I wanted to be moist red lips on a cracked china doll
I wanted to be shutters slamming on tempest nights
when the power is out
I wanted to be guttered candles and flickering torches
I wanted to be the thrill you feel at home by yourself
I wanted to be the realisation that you're not alone
I wanted to be hairs rising, goosebumps prickling
I wanted to be that whiplash look behind you
I wanted to be so much, so heightened, so fever-pitch scored
that you left the room, that you wished you could take more.

Jo Brandon

The Slammer

I had never left a meeting with a defendant so wholeheartedly worried than I had with Matt. Matt was incarcerated in HMP Maidstone on a petty theft charge, after making off with £110 from a convenience store. Far from a Bond villain, Matt was one of my many defendants in the region, and just like everyone else I had represented as a public defender, I assumed he would receive a short sentence of a few months and a fine. One morning, I was making my usual breakfast of poached eggs on white, when I received a call from the Kent Criminal Justice Board, alerting me that Matt was to be transferred elsewhere, due to an incident within the Maidstone prison. Unlike Matt I thought, but supposed he had been involved in an altercation that resulted in some sort of injury perhaps. I slipped a visit to see Matt in the new prison in my daily schedule, wedged between a visit to the courthouse, and a hearing for another defendant of mine. I would find out where he had been transferred during my visit to the courthouse.

"What do you mean I can't see him? Every defendant has the right to an attorney! It's unlawful for him to be locked up inside God knows where right up until his hearing." I barked at the clerk.

"I'm sorry sir, but I have direct orders from higher up not to release information regarding his whereabouts, until I am told to do so." My mouth sat open, my face visibly stunned, as I registered her sentence. Immediately as I left the building, I realised I could go to the papers with this, this was illegal. The court system is not allowed to stop you from seeing your client. I

dwelled on this for the remainder of the week, as I was bewildered and unsure about what to do next. If I went to the press, I would lose my opportunities to defend people, ergo my job. A few weeks had gone by, and I rang the courthouse weekly to see Matt, same answer every time.

One morning, I was making my usual breakfast of poached eggs on white, when I received a call to inform me that I was being removed from Matt's case, and another defence lawyer was being assigned. Their reason was that the case had become a lot more complicated, due to several incidents within incarceration, and thus, they required a more experienced lawyer. Now this was not uncommon, as I was fairly new and only represented those who had been accused of smaller crimes. I understood that perhaps someone with more experience should be defending Matt, but found it curious that I had not been allowed to visit these past few weeks.

Arrangements were made to meet with him one last time, at HMP Maidstone with his new defense lawyer. This was to transfer any documents I had, and get the new lawyer up to speed on the specifics of his case, something even I knew little about.

It was going relatively well, Matt had expressed that he had got into some fights with the guards and whatnot, but also unperturbed by the prospect of a new defendant - perhaps I had been overthinking his transfer. He seemed calm, composed, slightly tired, even drowsy. Nothing out of the ordinary, except that his demeanor was measured, almost as if he was being watched.

As the new lawyer left the interview room, Matt's eyes lit up. Remaining motionless in his movement, but erratic in his eyes, he began to scan the room.

"Listen to me, the guards in this new prison are sick bastards. They are putting on shows for the night staff, they're crazy lad!".

My eyebrows form a 'V' shape.

"What's that Matt? Remember you have to pass a drug test as part of your hearing, don't get involved with that crowd at your new place. Actually, where is your new place? The guards and the courthouse won't tell me for some reason." I replied, with an air of pity for his newfound hallucinations.

"Listen! The guards are making all the inmates perform stupid stuff, like a talent show, like juggling, magic, singing or anything mate, if anyone doesn't comply they get charges put on their records. It's the demented screws, they get a kick out of beating the shit out of anyone. I'm in HMP Abingdon, the building's so old and full of diseases!" As I sat listening to this, I couldn't help but remember other colourful tales I've been told during my time as a public defender. But somehow Matt's urgency seemed to me that he was telling the truth, I had never known him to be a conjurer of misinformation, I mean the guy was only picked up on a petty theft charge.

"HMP Abingdon is no longer in use, Matt, it hasn't been since the Second World War", I said hoping to put a bullet in the head of his story.

"That's it! I'm definitely in there mate, it's still got signs on the walls from the war. They set me up in Maidstone, and the Governor of the prison had it in for me, so they sent me to Abingdon. Honestly, I'm not lying, they make Terry from B Wing perform magic since he's a pickpocket, they make the hardest men in there sing like little girls! If anyone refuses they smack them

about, and we have to soak up the pools of blood! They add time to your sentence if you're shit, whilst the guards sit around drinking, smoking, laughing and banging their stick off the bars!" I couldn't comprehend his story. Was it even true, or just a farce? In a building that hasn't been used since the Second World War, they were transporting prisoners in for a brutal talent show, full of bloody beatdowns and beers for the late night guards? Suddenly he gripped my arms.

"Please, I need to get out," his voice breaks as he stares intensely, tears begin simmering in his eyes. I'm speechless, sitting with his tightening, vice-like grip on my forearms, contemplating my next sentence. It was clear this man had been tortured, that something had affected him inside the walls of Abingdon.

"Times up, let's go Matt," a guard said as he swiftly manoeuvered up to the table and began cuffing Matt. Matt's arms were down by his side as the guard opened the door, and his weird, hypnotic state had returned. I sat, absolutely confused at what he had said, and his change in demeanor in front of the staff. As he was led out of the room, his head turned to look back at me, almost robotically. His eyes were screaming with fear, but his body remained completely orderly. That was the last I had seen of Matt, and I knew I was no longer legally responsible for him.

One morning, I was making my usual breakfast of poached eggs on white, when I read the latest headline in the newspaper.

'FORMER PRISON OFFICER REVEALS INHUMANE TALENT SHOW IN ABANDONED PRISON'.

Oliver J. Campbell

Remember the Bear.

Do you remember the Bear in the Big Blue House?

How he used to push his giant wet nose against the screen, taking in your intoxicating scent before pulling back, resisting the temptation of the hunt.

Stopping himself for just a moment, before he pushes through the glass barricade, his jaw opening wide; releasing the heavy scent of rotting flesh.

Splinters of small, child-sized bones sticking out between his fangs, strings of ragged flesh in chunks stuck to his gums.

Pink tinged saliva dripping from his tongue, falling from his mouth; soaking into the living room carpet. His predatory gaze trained on you, pupils dilated at the thought of the feast of innocent young flesh he's about to devour.

Reducing you to nothing but a pool of blood slowly soaking into the carpeted floor for your mother to discover as soon as she's finished making lunch.

You know even if you screamed she wouldn't get to you in time, he'd be back on screen and you'd be gone.

So you sit there, paralysed. Eyes squeezed tight, breath held even tighter. Waiting for the end.

Moments pass...you hear the Bear's snuffling. You can almost feel his hot breath blowing over you then...

Nothing.

The Bear has pulled away now, telling you that you smell of grass as he moves on deeper into the house. You breathe a sigh of relief, realising you've survived another close encounter with The Bear.

There's always tomorrow though, you think. One day, your luck may run out...

Errol-Graham Harsley

No Strings Attached

I've been with him a lot since he died, inheriting his tormented fears. Pete Smith and I shared many things, but feeling his horror is making me crazy. My partner Christine is very concerned. It's something past three in the morning and I'm down here writing, trying to write it out of my system. I'm on medication. Christine will raise hell if she finds me here at this time. Me, Phil Jones, on medication. No strings attached.

It all started when we were kids in the last year of primary school, the fad then was Pelham string puppets. I had a Teddy, Pete had Looby Loo and a lad called Joey Gibson had Andy Pandy. The Pandy family at school, like the TV series, should have been innocent. As we got to know Gibson neither Pete or I liked him, he was cruel and would pull the legs off spiders and cut earthworms up into pieces. Horrible. All of the vile acts he committed were executed with him pretending to be an Andy Pandy puppet. Along with having a Pandy striped blue hat, Gibson's evil was always accompanied by an inane grin fastened to his face. Innocent family of puppets made evil. Gibson so twisted, evil.

I sort of stood up to Gibson if he'd start on me, but Pete, Looby Loo, was a gentle boy, artistic, softly spoken and therefore frequently picked on, often being called: queer, bum boy, homo. Pete was a lovely kid who grew up to be a lovely man. Anyway, at school the three of us would put on a show for the infants on wet play times. The puppets dancing to records in front of the curtain in the hall. The teacher would then get the little ones dancing, burning off excessive energy. The puppets lived in an old picnic basket at the side of the stage. One day Pete and I discovered that the strings on both our puppets had been cut. There was a note in the box:

No strings attached. No Teddy, no Looby Loo, now whatever is to happen to you?

Andy Pandy wasn't there. We were distraught and told our teacher Mr Davies, who just shook his head in dismay saying out-loud the boy's name: 'Joey Gibson'. I hear Christine cough upstairs. Hope she returns to sleep without missing me. Hell to pay. On medication. Gibson? I sort of stood up to him. No strings attached.

Shortly after the damage to our puppets, Pete suffered a meeting with Gibson and two of his mates. It was getting dark and Pete and his dog were heading home. The three lads approached. Gibson, wearing the same grin, was playing puppet, his juvenile rhyme of words and childlike voice announced Andy Pandy:

"Oh, sweet sweet Pete, that's who we meet on the street." As he was speaking Gibson moved closer to Pete, the finger and thumb of his right-hand making scissor movements in front of him and his dog. The flesh that would be scissors hovered around Pete's face.

"Teddy gone, no Looby Loo, now whatever is to happen to you? No strings attached, cut here, cut there, but no, no joke, lets us in the eyes sweet Pete poke."

Gibson's fingers and thumb swung down to Pete's face and plunged into his eyes. Pete shouted out in pain. The dog barked. Gibson's mates laughed. Pete turned and started to run, the dog yelping in pain as Joey's boot arrived on its backside.

For Pete, there were to be many similar incidents over the coming years 'till Gibson moved on finding even more evil. He graduated in his teens to shooting cats with his air rifle, involved in gang violence, did time for GBH and was eventually killed by his girlfriend. She did humanity a favour. One of the worst and last incidents regarding Pete was him finding his pet rabbit with both of its ears cut off; the whole run saturated in blood and the rabbit lying dead. Pinned to the netting was the message:

No strings attached, Teddy gone, Rabbit too, now whatever is to happen to you?

Pete did well, went to art college and ended up teaching. He met Wendy, bought a nice house and tried to forget the past. Something lingered, Joey Gibson, although dead, lingered. Pete had dreams, night scares.

Then the cancer. That flawed us all, first they thought it curable. They opened Pete up and it had spread, palliative care at home was all there was. I visited regularly watching him fade and edge towards death. After he'd gone, I was contacted by his Macmillan nurse. She said that she was disturbed by what Pete had told her. In the dark of night he had heard footsteps coming up the stairs. The door had slowly opened bringing light from the landing to present a skeletal Gibson donned in Pandy paraphernalia of blue and white stripes. The marionette plodded its way into the room, making scissor-like movements with both hands.

Gibson at first had quietly sung:

"Andy Pandy's coming to play, lah la lah la lahla

Andy Pandy's here today, lah, lahla lah."

And then talked in his twisted child-like manner:

"Sweet, sweet Pete, beneath a sheet, how nice again it is to meet. I'll sever your strings one by one and I can promise you'll be gone. No strings attached, evil, only evil to be hatched!"

Pete was on morphine, but what he said did, well it did, sound convincing. She then added that Pandy, Gibson or whoever it was had said:

"And to your friend Philip Jones, I'll soon be playing with his bones."

She said, he said.

I sort of stood up to him.

Pete on morphine, I'm on medication. Shouldn't be sitting down here.

Noises on the stairs.

Christine, she'll be angry with me.

Christine?

Not Christine.

Definitely not Christine.

A faint voice:

"Andy Pandy's coming to play, lah la lah la lahla

Andy Pandy's here today, lah, lahla lah."

Alan G. Smith

But Emily Loved Him.

He stalked me to the front door, which I opened violently. "I need some fresh air. Goodbye," I snapped, wanting him to know I resented having to explain my whereabouts. The pompous bastard insisted on manners and etiquette, although my contract didn't actually stipulate good moods as an essential skill of the role.

"Fresh air, my arse" I muttered, and hurried off in the direction of the village pub with inebriation on my mind. It was worrying, the way he encroached on my private life. No other pet sitting job had caused me such anxiety. All animals and their owners could be tricky, for sure—dubious stroking rituals, 'personal' cleaning—still, he was the first to demand electronic tagging. The clunky ankle device tracked my every move.

It wasn't right. A girl had to have fun, after all. Indulging in a little weekend relaxation with my pal Stella Artois was my business and nothing to do with my saggy old boss.

I looked behind to see if he was following. Thankfully the dark streets were empty. "It'll be okay. Don't be a wuss," I told myself, quite firmly, and stepped into the foggy loveliness of The Stag. Engulfed by beery laughing, I soon forget pretty much everything except whether or not I could get in another five pints and if there would be time for fish and chips, pickled egg on the side.

Four pints and a shot later, the world was good. 'Yeah, I'm up for it,' I told Hairy Bill confidently, offering up my hand for the weekly arm-wrestling competition.

He grinned and rolled up his sleeves. "You feeling lucky, Em?"

"Feeling lucky. You're my best friend," I hiccupped, by way of answer. I rubbed around his legs three times before I realised what I was doing. Picking up animal habits went with the territory for us pet sitters.

Something flitted past the window. It was gone in a striped-pink haze, too quickly for me to be sure.

It wasn't him; it wasn't him, I told myself. You're safe here. It's not curfew hour yet.

Blinking rapidly to clear the vision, I leaned across the table and licked Bill's salt and vinegar forehead. "Ready."

He reared back, shouting about cheating and then we started the wrestle.

I used everything I'd got, which was very little. Within seconds, Bill had my arm trapped. "OK, OK. You win." I gasped.

He laughed crazily and planted a kiss on my cheek. Though I had been sweet on him for some time, a drunken fumble was not enough to force out the image of the baggy pink thing that had shot past the window. Determined to ignore it, I pushed my way through the crowds to the bar, and downed another pint.

I stayed until closing time, flirting with Hairy Bill and singing all the ballads. In the heady rush, I forgot the curfew and my promise to my employer that I would be back before midnight.

Arms around each other, me and Bill staggered round the back of the pub. "Whas' the time?"

"Urgh," Bill replied, and then a lot happened, in flashes of fluffy pink. Hairy Bill tried to fight our attacker but he was no match for the cloth paw—a bit loose at the seams—that soon had his helpless body pinned to the floor. His screams made my employer more excited.

"Don't make a sound, Hairy Bill! He's marking his territory. Roll over and admit defeat and he'll let you go."

As predicted, the instant the strapping fella scrambled onto his back, arms and legs in the air, my boss stopped yowling and the danger was over. All that was left was for the domineering bugger to climb over Bill's shaking body.

"Same time next weekend?" I called, as the smell of cat piss pervaded the air and I was lifted up in the mouth of the gigantic furry feline. The last I saw of Bill was his terrified face and the puddle of pee.

Despite being made of cloth, Bagpuss's teeth were an iron grip. I protested. "I was on my way home! It's not my fault my watch has broken. There was no need to attack Hairy Bill like that! Why do you always have to pee on my friends?"

By the time we reached home, I had accepted my lot and became docile. I held my arms straight ahead in readiness for the plunge through the cat flap, knowing from bitter experience that elbows and feet could impede our journey.

Gently, the old cloth cat maneuvered us into the kitchen, only placing me down once we reached the carpet. "Baggy bastard," I said, affectionately, scratching behind his pink and yellow striped ears until he purred. "Too old for those games, Mister. What are you going to do once your head falls off? Eh?"

I stroked his head until he yawned and closed his eyes. "But Emily loved him," I whispered into his battered ear and snuggled down to sleep.

Claire Hinchliffe

Home Again

She was standing at the step leading to the outer door of the house, watching the keyhole poised like pursed lips, ready to bite. There was no one else to clean out the house and reluctantly she had resigned herself to the task in hand. Drawing a breath, she tentatively pushed the door ajar. Superficially, the house was unremarkable, impersonating a quiet life. Yet, behind its façade, Number 39 looked like an *Emerald City* erected from abandoned *Gordon's* bottles, cardboard boxes and rusting cans. The house reintroduced itself with a smell - raw and rotten like grief. She closed the door and leant back against it. Even amongst the wreckage, she felt a faint sense of bewilderment; she had imagined it all being much bigger - remembered taller ceilings, a wider awning, a longer hall. But it was hard to feel nostalgic surrounded by all of this decay.

Clambering through the house, her hands pushed back objects like the low hanging branches in a wood, until she reached the kitchen. She put her bag and coat down on a square of tissue, a cordon sanitaire she had designated on the grimy worksurface. She took three paracetamol and started to fill black bin bags. The floor was horizontal with things. She pulled them open like drawers or cupboards, inspecting the contents: a hundred and fifty-eight *Blue Peter* badges, a suitcase full of red milk bottle tops, indistinguishable meat-like cubes crawling with tiny maggots, nineteen personal stereos in a disintegrating *Woolworths* bag, unopened bags of crisps and all of them discontinued flavours. The house reverberated around her. It seemed to be breathing, exhaling with the relief of a person inside it. The tins of food had been there so long their insides had vanished and their grey skeletons were crumbling. Cockroaches scuttled past her hands as she tied bag after bag. By the time one corner of the room was clear, she stood with the backs of her hands on her hips, watching. The refracted light flickered with rainbow colours, but the empty window seat unsettled her. It was so still, like nothing had ever happened there.

Upstairs, the rooms had changed. The bedrooms were full, floor to ceiling, windows to walls. They were in fact, so full, artefacts had clumped together to create new walls and sinuous pathways from room to room. Yet, even under the weight of the wheezing house, her mother's bedroom seemed the same. She removed the bed clothes. She boxed up a pile of shoes, unable to fathom why they were all odd. Pausing and looking at the wardrobe, it was hard not to feel mocked by the memory that she had once kept her clothes in there, at a time when she had more things than her mother. She barely needed to open the wardrobe to uncover her mother's pale rain mac; the one she always wore, her favourite coat. It was a light yellowish-fawn colour like the complexion of a china doll. She'd been wearing it the last night they saw each other. It seemed important to remove it from the other familiar clothes and display it on the wardrobe door. It hung there. Strung up by its neck, suspended by sinewy threads and the echo of her body, such a sleepy little ghost. She looked and looked at it, until her eyes started to blur as it became skin. She remembered that as a child she learned that the lion in *The Wizard of Oz* wore a costume made from the hide and fur of a real lion. Perhaps this too was more than a costume? It took the shape she remembered; wide at the hips with a smaller waist. Through her squinting eyes, maybe, she could even see the birthmark on the shoulder. It appeared sensible that the police might have tidied her mother away, after the coroner's inquest, a pair of lungs in the bathroom cabinet, a rhythmic heart in the kitchen sink. She put it on.

Back downstairs, she unpacked the bags of debris around her: re-stacking the tins of *Campbell's* soup with sell-by dates from before the millennium, piling up old *Vogue* magazines in the corner, re-towering the hair extensions and wigs upon the washing machine. The house inhaled. A rat ran along the skirting board. She locked eyes with her glassy twin in the mirrored pane of the back door. The coat twinkled in the early evening light, like wet skin. She threw handfuls of costume jewellery across the hallway floor, fashioning a road. She ordered the cracked faces of china dolls along the ironing board for company. The house rattled, like it might fall on her, crush her with its great beam and leave nothing more than her two feet sticking out. The thought was amusing. She turned on all the taps and every light. She opened the windows and all the doors. The house gasped. She lit a handful of candles and ripped every bin liner open at the seams. Then, she sat down with her legs outstretched, allowing the cascade of things to pour themselves around her. And with the clapping of her heels, she started to laugh to herself, "There's no place like home".

Stella Miriam Pryce

Spiders

"Don't listen to that programme again,"
my mother said, coming into the kitchen
to find me huddled on the table

as if huddling on a table could save me
from spiders bigger than houses,
huge bodies, enormous eyes,

terrible eight legs, and venom.
Their strength was unbelievable.
They were trampling over the world.

They wanted to rule the world
and they didn't care about humans.
"Turn that radio off - it's tea-time."

But I couldn't switch it off.
I couldn't stop listening
to the terrifying spiders.

Sarah Barr

Three Matches

The blackness was absolute.

It bore down like the weight of the Earth, swaddling him in an indelible cocoon. For several long moments he wasn't sure if his eyes were open or closed.

Have I gone blind?

The silence roared in his ears. *Have I gone deaf?*

Reaching out in reflex, his knuckles rapped against a solid surface with a bloom of pain, leaving skin behind. A swell of panic compressed his chest and as he gulped in a greedy breath of stale air, his meaty stomach pressed into the same unyielding barrier.

He began to search with his hands, squirming, pushing and probing. A fat bead of sweat trickled across his temple, despite the cold. Slowly, he explored the inside of his tiny tomb.

He patted his flesh. *Why am I naked?*

Hello? He called. Nothing. The blackness swallowed his voice.

He hugged himself. A barrier of crossed arms against the nothing.

An object. His fingers stumbled across a tiny object laid on his flabby chest and he clutched it like a lifeline. A fold of card with a slim strip that abraded his fingers; three frail sticks inside. A matchbook.

Fumbling, he tore out a match and awkwardly held the book to his face. *If I could see, everything would be better.*

He pawed the match across the strip once. Again. For a third time. It flared, brighter than a fragment of the sun caught in a jar. Immediately he squeezed his eyes shut in agony & wheezed frantically at the tiny flame.

The spark went out. The acrid stench of its passing hung in the stagnant air. It's afterimage clung like a scar to the inside of his eyelids.

It was a while before the temptation returned.

It would be foolish, he admonished, *to waste another match.*

Matches, he reminded himself, *require oxygen.*

So do you, he hissed.

But every thought returned insatiably to the second match. He lay in the darkness, cuddling the matchbook.

Wouldn't it be better if I could see?

Perhaps, he reasoned, *it would be worth spending a little oxygen.*

Only this time, he conceded, *be ready.*

Titillated, he peeled back the matchbook's flimsy covering.

Pulling out the second match, he carefully screwed his eyes tight shut before he struck it. He perceived an orange blossom beyond his eyelids and, ever so gradually, cracked open his eyes.

He was imprisoned in pale plywood.

His vision swam through indulgent tears and stinging, pooled sweat. There was something there; a blurry message scrawled on the coarse, bare surface. And a pale square. A polaroid. It was too close and his aging eyes refused to focus.

He yelped as the match burned unnoticed into his fingertips and the light sputtered out.

You have to see.

The darkness flooded back and embraced him like an unwelcome lover, heavy, cloying & relentless.

You have to know.

Feverishly he rubbed the last match against the strip over and over, feeling it go limp & crumple between his clammy fingers. His entire existence shrunk to one goal:

Read the message. Understand.

Shaking, he braced the bulbous tip of the match with his forefinger and swept it hard across the ignition strip. A sob of relief burst from his throat as the final match fizzled to life.

Pushing with the bare soles of his feet, he crammed his head into the corner of the box and forced his face as far away from the writing as possible. His treacherous eyes burned with effort.

Rows of pinched faces stared out from the picture taped above the letters. Striped ties and uniform navy blazers. His own face beamed out from the back row, bracketed by his closest cronies and encircled in bright red ink.

With the last of the light, his gaze travelled down to the letters. Painfully, slowly they settled into shape.

You wont be missed

L Hudson

About Greenteeth Press

Greenteeth Press is a small, independent publisher committed to representing readers and writers from all backgrounds, with books, pamphlets, and anthologies - making books accessible for all. Inspired by the landscapes and folklore in the North of England, their first anthology, Pondweed, was published in August 2019.

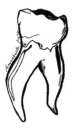

Greenteeth Press' logo was designed & illustrated by Julia King.

Julia can be found on Etsy at JuliasPrintStudio on Etsy, via Instagram at @JuliasPrintStudio.

About York Centre for Writing

Horrifying Tales is a collaboration between Greenteeth Press and the Horrifying Children: children's television, literature and popular culture project, curated by Robert Edgar, John Marland and Lauren Stephenson and is part of the York Centre for Writing.

The York Centre for Writing is based in the School of Humanities at York St John University. It serves as a hub for a number of exciting writing events, projects and publications, including partnership with the York Literature Festival. The centre hosts a range of degree programmes, including undergraduate degrees in Creative Writing and in Literature, MA degree programmes in Creative Writing, in Literature and in Publishing, an MFA in Creative Writing and practice-based PhDs.

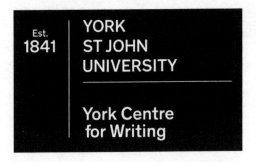

@ysjwriting

blog.yorksj.ac.uk/creativewriting/

Publisher's Acknowledgements

Greenteeth Press would like to thank the writers who submitted their work to this anthology, entrusting us with their time and efforts.

York St John University have been a vital asset to the production of Horrifying Tales, particularly Dr Robert Edgar for sharing his proffessional knowledge and being an excellent creative partner on this project.

We thank the Publishing MA cohort at YSJ and Iona Dickinson for their editorial suggestions and time spent proofreading.

We thank Dan Hunt for perfectly capturing our vision in his cover design and for his time spent managing our social media accounts.